The Tin-Pot Foreign General and the Old Iron Woman

RAYMOND BRIGGS

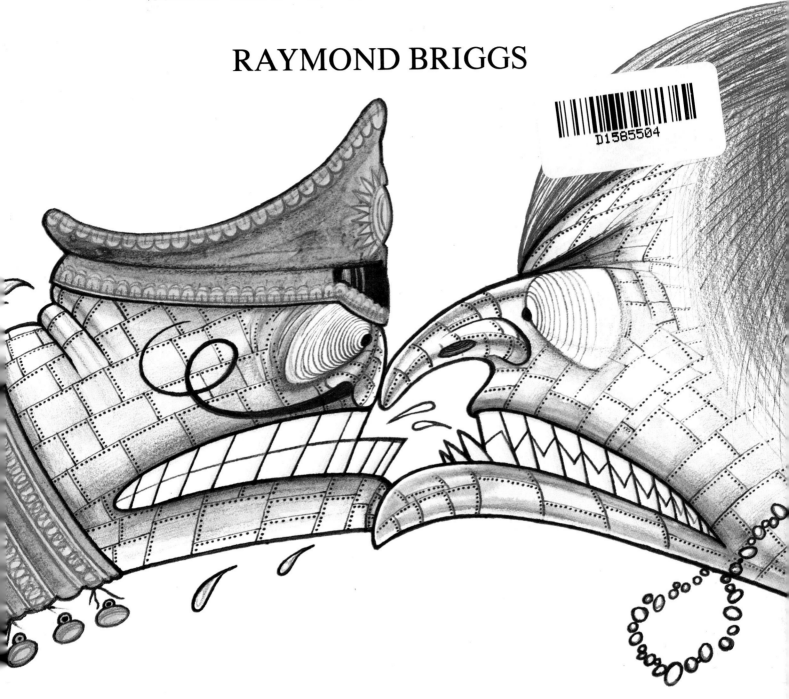

HAMISH HAMILTON
London

Nationalism is an infantile disease.
It is the measles of mankind.
ALBERT EINSTEIN

Patriotism is the last refuge of a scoundrel.
DR. JOHNSON

First published in Great Britain 1984 by
Hamish Hamilton Ltd
Garden House 57–59 Long Acre London WC2E 9JZ
Copyright © 1984 by Raymond Briggs
All rights reserved

British Library Cataloguing in Publication Data
Briggs, Raymond
    The tinpot foreign general and the old iron woman.
    I. Title
    823'.914[F]   PR6052.R444/
    Hardback ISBN 0-241-11362-8
    Paperback ISBN 0-241-11363-6

Colour separations by Dot Gradations
Printed in Great Britain by
Redwood Burn Ltd, Trowbridge, Wiltshire.

Once upon a time, down at the bottom of the world, there was a sad little island.

No one lived on the sad little island except for a few poor shepherds.
These poor shepherds spent all their time

counting their sheep and eating them.
They had mutton for breakfast, mutton for dinner
and mutton for tea.

Next door to the sad little island was a great big kingdom, ruled over by a Wicked Foreign General.

This Wicked Foreign General had wicked foreign
moustachios, and although he had lots of gold on
his hat, he was not real. He was made of Tin Pots.

Now, this Tin-Pot Foreign General wanted to be Important. He wanted to do something Historical, so that his name would be printed in all the big History Books.

So, one day, he got all his soldiers and all his guns
and he put them into boats. Then he sailed them
over the sea to the sad little island.

There he stamped ashore and bagsied the sad little island for his very own.

The poor shepherds did not like this at all, because the Tin-Pot Foreign General started bossing them about.

Now listen! Far away over the sea there lived
an old woman with lots of money and guns.

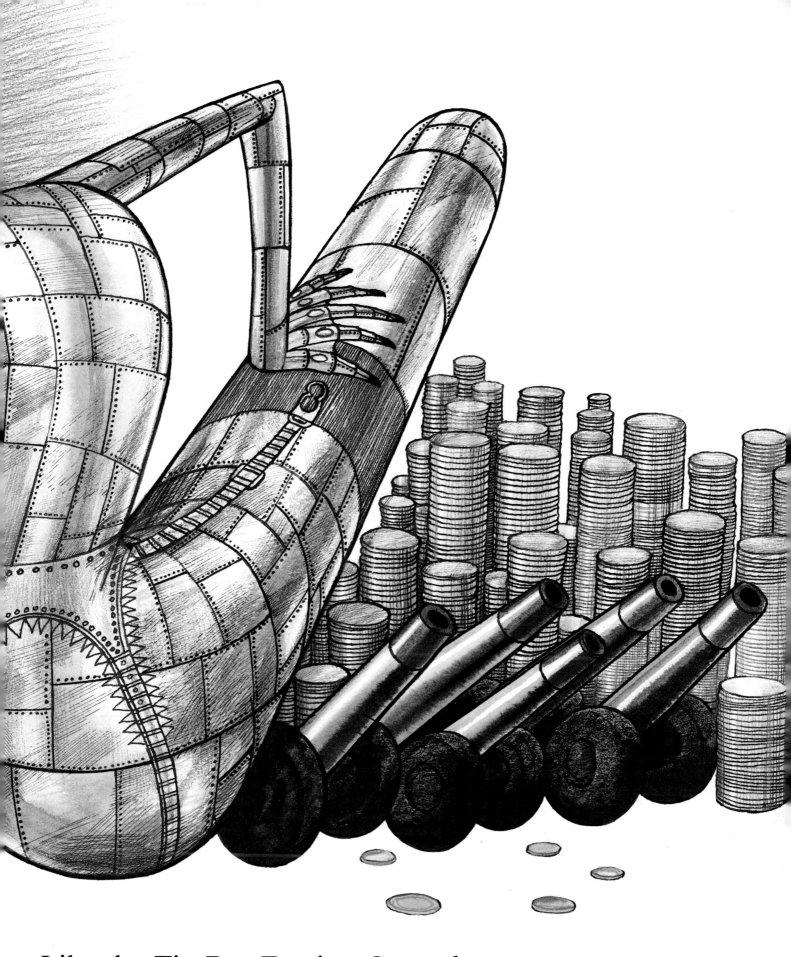

Like the Tin-Pot Foreign General,
she was not real, either. She was made of Iron.

When this Old Iron Woman heard that the Tin-Pot
Foreign General had bagsied the sad little island,
she flew into a rage.

"It's MINE!" she screeched."MINE! MINE! MINE!
I bagsied it AGES ago! I bagsied it FIRST!
DID! DID! DID!"

She poured out tons of treasure from her
huge chest and bought lots and lots of boats.

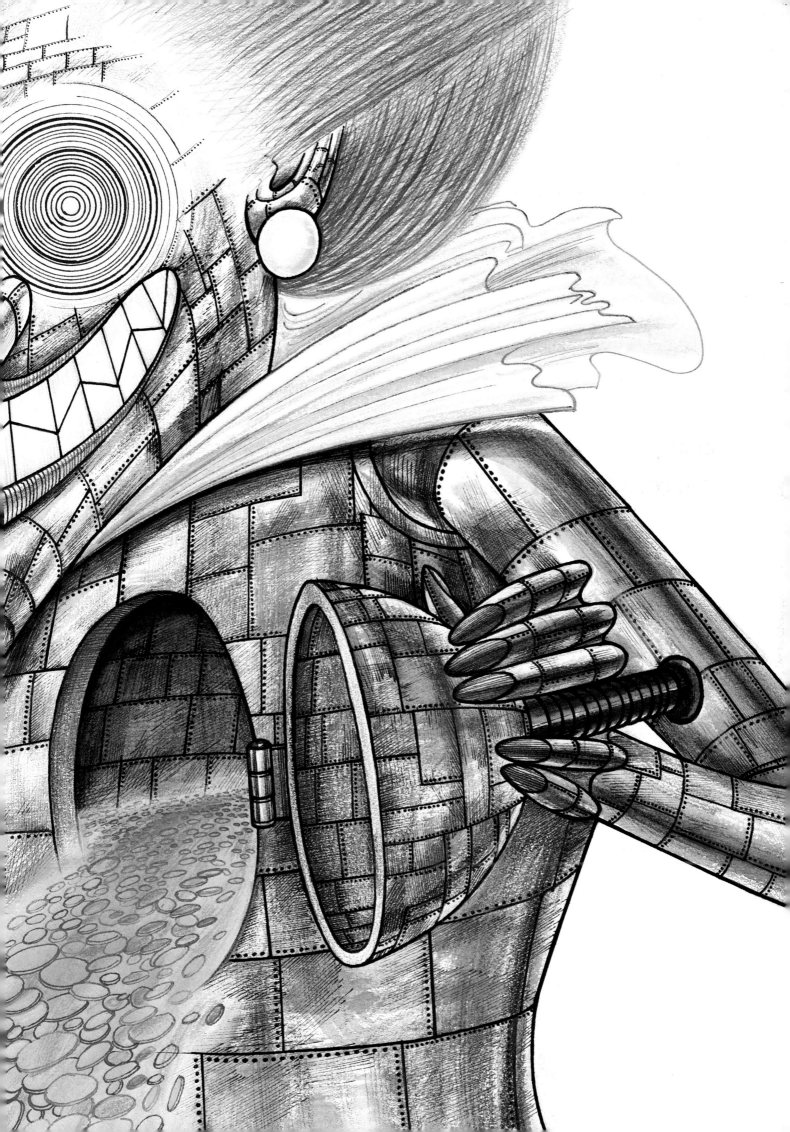

Then she got all her soldiers and guns and she put them into the boats and sailed them over the sea to the sad little island.

She wanted to bagsy the sad little island back again,
you see.

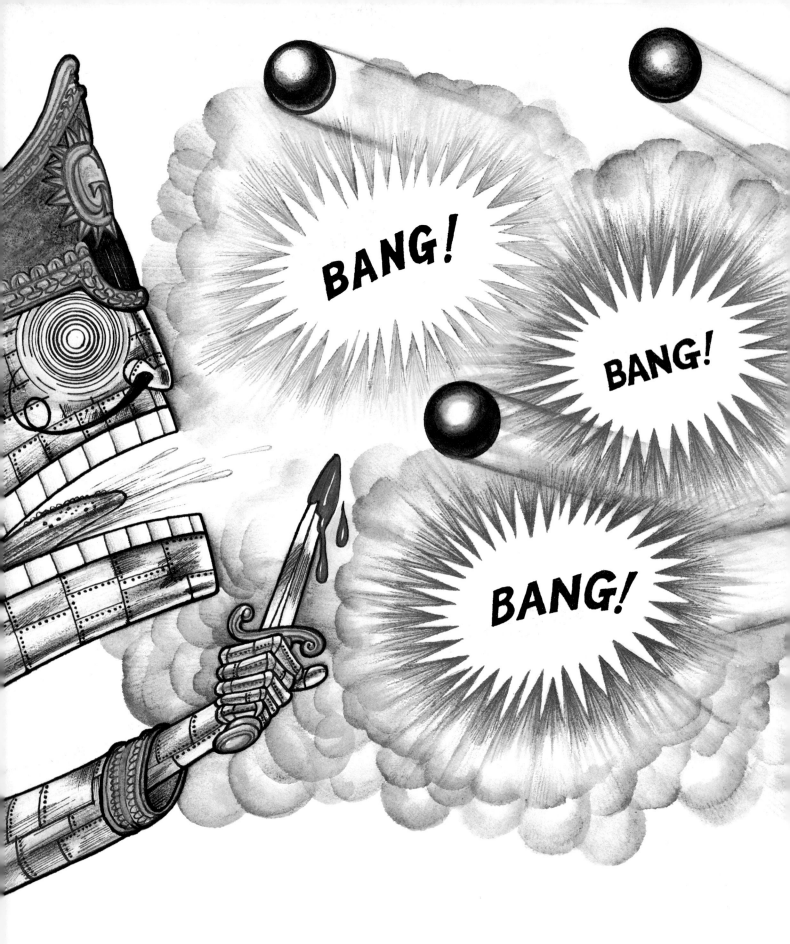

BANG! BANG! BANG!
went the guns of the Tin-Pot Foreign General.

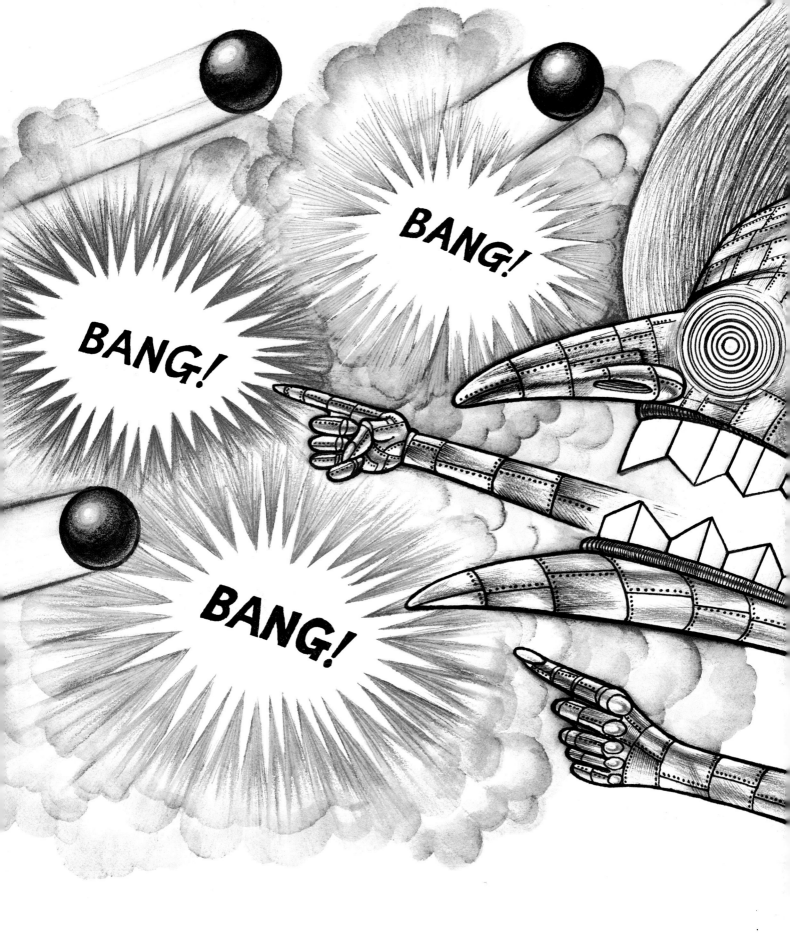

BANG! BANG! BANG!
went the guns of the Old Iron Woman.

Some men were shot.

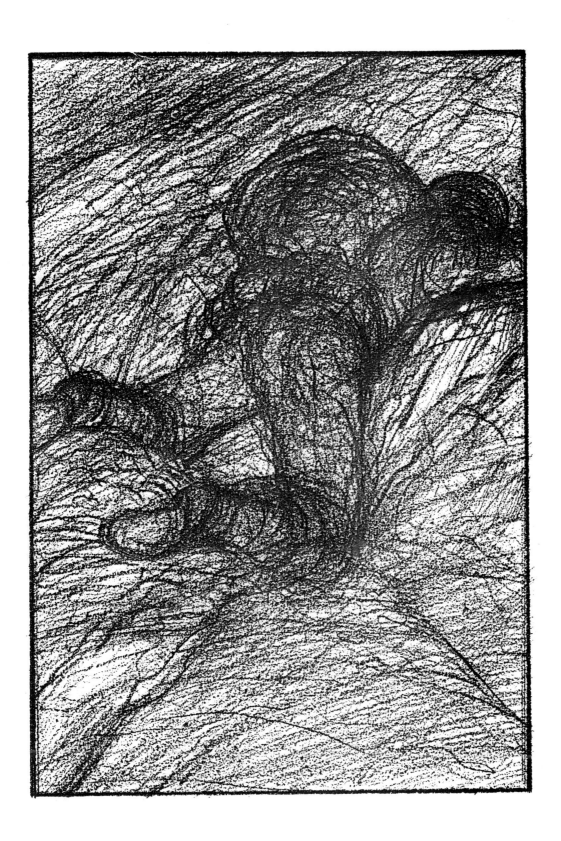

Some men were drowned.

Some men were burned alive.

Some men were blown to bits.

Some men were only half blown to bits and

came home with parts of their bodies missing.

Hundreds of brave men were killed. And the

...ere all real men, made of flesh and blood.
They were not made of Tin or of Iron.

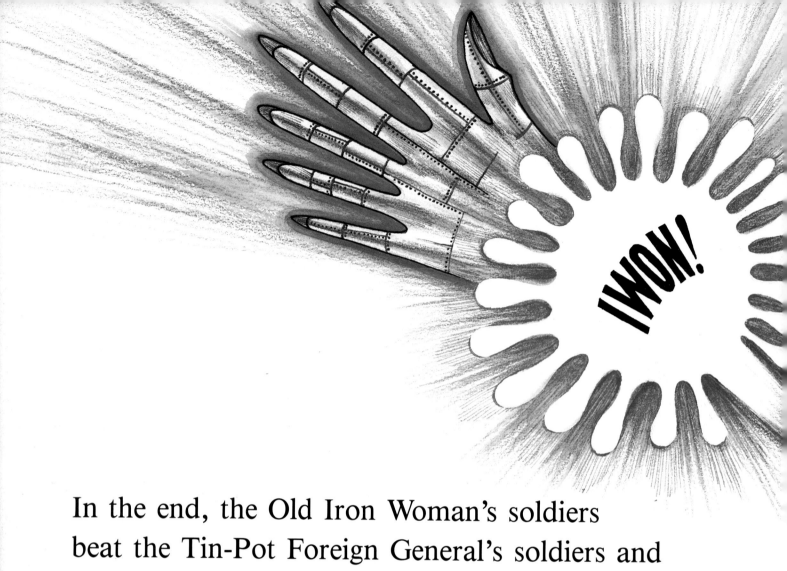

In the end, the Old Iron Woman's soldiers
beat the Tin-Pot Foreign General's soldiers and
the Tin-Pot Foreign General's soldiers ran away.

"I WON!" sang the Old Iron Woman. "REJOICE!"

"Mei villi ritorno!" (I will return!) swore the
Tin-Pot Foreign General.

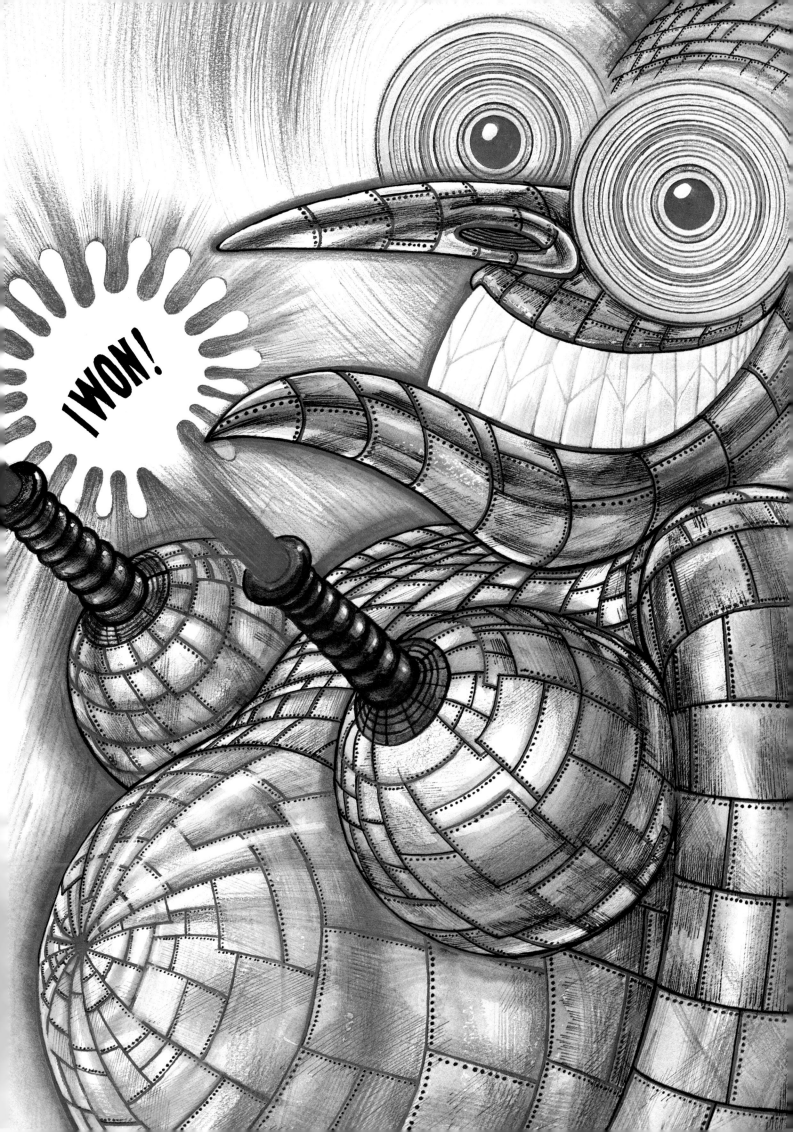

So the poor shepherds on the sad little island went
on counting their sheep and eating them.
They had mutton for breakfast, mutton for dinner

and mutton for tea.
Three of them were killed in the battle, but no one
was to blame.

Later on, a boat came back to the Old Iron Woman'

...ingdom with a big iron box full of dead bodies.

Then the Old Iron Woman gave all her soldier

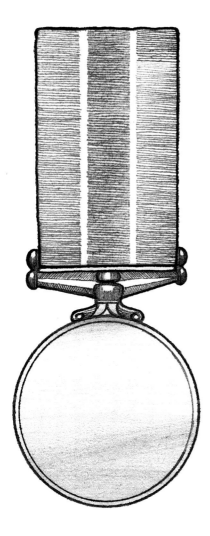

special medal.

After this, there was a Grand Parade to celebrate the Grea

Victory and everyone went to Church and Thanked God.

But the soldiers with bits of their bodies missing were not invited to take part in the Grand Parade, in case the sight of them spoiled the rejoicing. Some watched from a grandstand and others stayed at home with their memories and their medals.

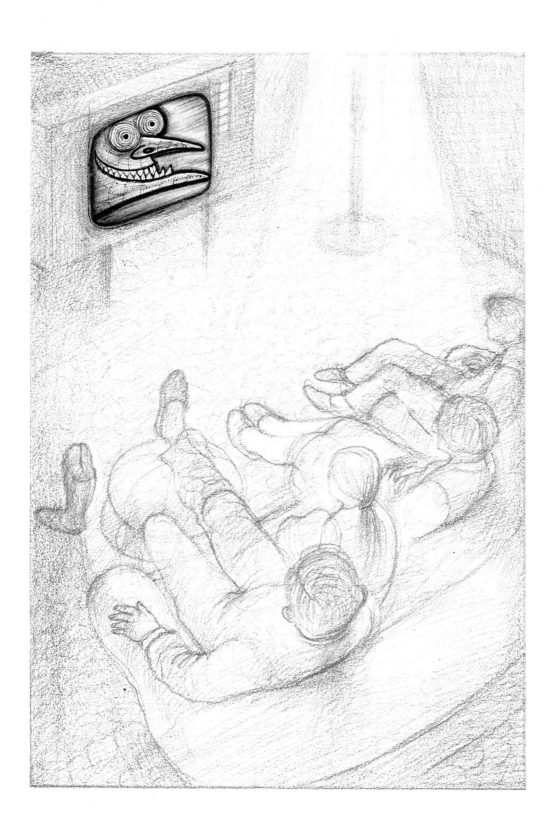

And the families of the dead tended the graves.